I'm SAD When...

Anabell Segura Lanz

I'm sad when I feel lonely.

I’m sad when
I lose something important.

I'm sad when plans change unexpectedly.

I’m sad when big people shout.

I'm sad when I get hurt.

I’m sad when I break my favourite toy.

I'm sad when it's raining and
I can't play outside.

I'm sad when others are unkind.

I'm sad when mum or dad get sick.

COCO

I’m sad when we fight.

I’m sad when I lose a best pet friend.

COCO

I'm sad when
I have to say goodbye.

I’m sad when others feel sad.

I know I am sad because:

My body is tired
and I have no energy
I sometimes
feel like crying
My
shoulders
slouch
My smile
is upside
down
I don't
stand up
tall

What makes you sad?

(Draw it here)

Anabell Segura Lanz

Anabell was born in Venezuela but lives in Madrid, Spain. From her small studio she started her illustration project aNi ilustra, through which she enjoys creating colorful illustrations and stories that allow her to connect with the emotions of little readers.

I'm Sad When... is her second book as author-illustrator, and is part of a series in which she invites you to recognise your emotions in the small moments of everyday life.

Visit her online at **aniilustra.com or @aniilustra on Instagram.**